Pierogi

Fatayer

BEEF PATTY

JAMAICAN

Ravioli

Pierogi

BAO

Tamale

BAO

Ravioli

Fatayer

Pierogi

Tamale

JAMAICAN

BEEF PATTY

PATTY

BAO

Pierogi

Pierogi

Fatayer

JAMAICAN

BEEF PATTY

Fatayer

Ravioli

Pierogi

Pierogi

BAO

Tamale

BAO

Ravioli

Fatayer

Pierogi

JAMAICAN

Tamale

Dumplings for Lili

Dumplings for Lili

MELISSA IWAI

Norton Young Readers

An Imprint of W. W. Norton & Company
Independent Publishers Since 1923

"Lili, do you want to help me make baos?"

It's a special day
when Nai Nai says,

Of course, I say, "YES!"

Baos are bundles of warm,
doughy, juicy yumminess!

They are my favorite food
in the whole world.

I love making them.
My Nai Nai taught me all
the secrets to happy and
delicious baos.

SECRET #1 Mix the flour, yeast, sugar, oil, and water together and let them make friends.

SECRET #2 Knead the dough lovingly but firmly until it is as smooth as a baby's cheek. Let it take a catnap in a warm place while you make the filling.

SECRET #3 Thank the filling ingredients for growing strong and healthy as you mince and grate them.

SECRET #4 Shake the wok energetically and watch the filling dance with joy.

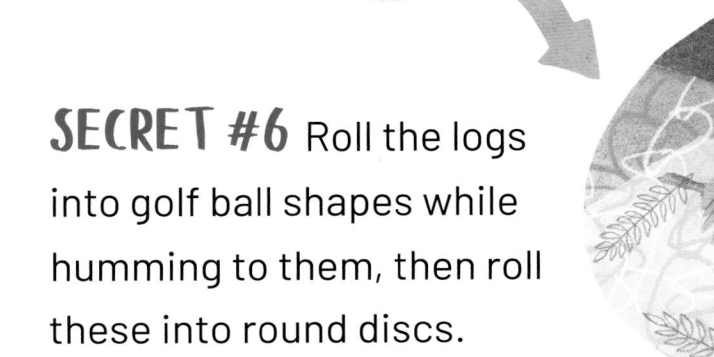

SECRET #5 Make a hole in the center of the dough and squeeze and pull it to make a large ring. Carefully cut it into cute mini logs.

SECRET #6 Roll the logs into golf ball shapes while humming to them, then roll these into round discs.

SECRET #7 (the most important and most difficult!) Gently spoon filling onto the dough. Coax it into the center and wrap it up snugly in its doughy blanket, pinching edges (at least 10 times!) and gathering at the top.

The last secret—**SECRET #8**—is to line the basket
with cabbage leaves before steaming so that
the bao babies don't stick to the bottom.

"Zao gao!" Nai Nai exclaims. "We are out of cabbage!"

Nai Nai asks me to see if Babcia on the 6th floor
of our building has any cabbage we can use.

Kiki and I say, "We'll be right back!"
and rush out to the elevator.

Oh no!

We skip up the five flights of stairs
to Babcia's apartment.

"Lili!" exclaims Babcia. "Of course I have cabbage
for your baos!" She hands me a giant head in a bag.

"But I was just about to make pierogi before you came,
and do licha! My potatoes are growing little
sprouts out of their eyes!" she says.

Suddenly her face lights up.
"Do you think you could do me a favor and
borrow some potatoes from Granma on the 2nd floor?"

"No problem, Babcia! We'll be right back!"
I call out as Kiki and I hop

down

the four flights of stairs

to Granma's apartment.

"Howdeedo, Lili!" Granma says and gives me a big hug.

"Of course I have some potatoes for Babcia's pierogi!"
she says. She hands me two large ones.

"But I was in the middle of making beef patties,
when, Cha! I noticed my garlic is all shriveled
and wrinkled," she sighs.

"Would you be a dear and ask if Abuela on the
4th floor would lend me some fresh garlic?"

I could never say no to Granma,
    so Kiki and I trot back up the stairs
        to give Babcia her potatoes . . .

. . . and we gallop down two
    flights to Abuela's apartment.

"Hola, Lili!" says Abuela.
She is happy to lend Granma a whole head of fresh garlic.

As Kiki and I are about to leave, she says, "¡O, cielos!
I'm out of cumin! How will I finish making my tamales?"

I remember that Nonna on the 3rd floor has lots of
spices in her kitchen. "Don't worry, Abuela," I say.
"Kiki and I will go ask Nonna for cumin!"

We rush downstairs to Granma's
    to give her the head of garlic,
        then off we go to Nonna's.

"Buongiorno, Lili!" Nonna says, dusting off her hands.
We go inside to Nonna's cozy kitchen. She searches
in her cupboard for a jar of cumin. "Cumin I have,"
says Nonna. "Here, give this to Abuela."

"Cavoli!" she exclaims. "I am all out of olive oil!
How will I make a sauce for my ravioli?"

Kiki and I exchange glances. . . .

"Lili, can you do me a big favor and ask Teta
upstairs if she has some olive oil to spare?"

I trudge up to the 4th floor
    to give the cumin to Abuela.

Kiki watches.

"Gracias, mi amor!" says Abuela.

Then it's up to the 5th
to Teta's.

Teta's kitchen smells heavenly. She is making fatayer.
She gives me some olive oil to take to Nonna.

Kiki and I take a deep breath.

Down the stairs we fly to Nonna.

Nonna is so happy she can finish making her ravioli.
I just want to finish making our bao!

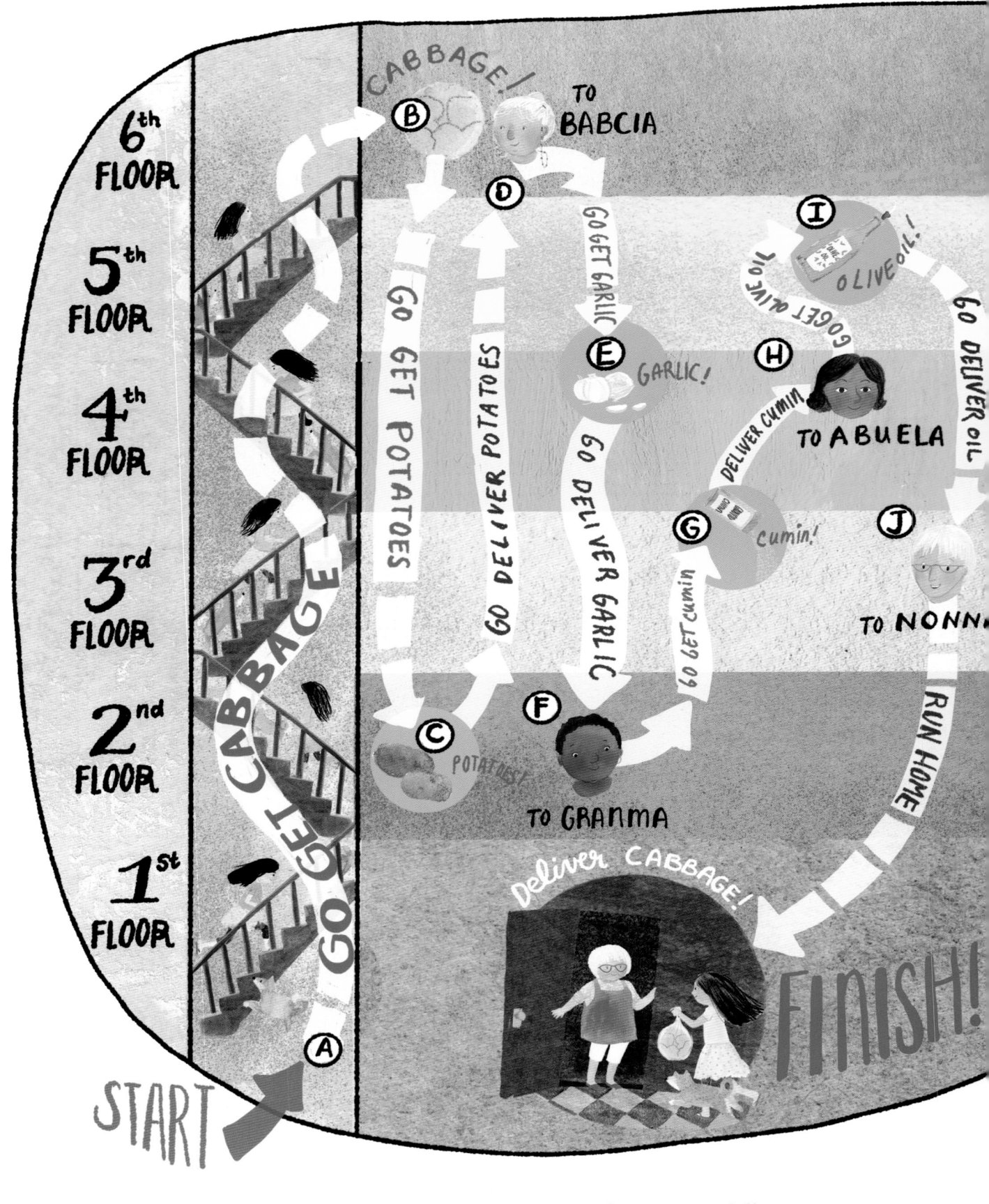

6th FLOOR

5th FLOOR

4th FLOOR

3rd FLOOR

2nd FLOOR

1st FLOOR

CABBAGE!

Ⓑ TO BABCIA

Ⓓ

GO GET GARLIC

Ⓔ GARLIC!

GO GET POTATOES

GO DELIVER POTATOES

GO DELIVER GARLIC

Ⓒ POTATOES!

Ⓕ TO GRANMA

GO GET CABBAGE

GO GET CUMIN

Ⓖ Cumin!

DELIVER CUMIN

Ⓗ TO ABUELA

GO GET OLIVE OIL

Ⓘ OLIVE OIL!

GO DELIVER OIL

Ⓙ TO NONNA

RUN HOME

Deliver CABBAGE!

START

Ⓐ

FINISH!

We clatter all the way back down to the ground floor.

I tell Nai Nai all about our adventures while we tuck our baby baos into the steamer basket lined with Babcia's cabbage leaves.

Later we go outside. We bring our freshly steamed bao.
The other grandmothers come with their little dumpling treasures.

Babcia with
her pierogi,

Granma with her beef patties,

Abuela with
her tamales,

Nonna with her ravioli,

Teta with her fatayer.

And the best treasure of all . . .

It's a big dumpling party!

. . . Mama and Papa come home with my new baby brother.

Now I have another little dumpling treasure!

NAI NAI's BAOS

MAKES 10 BAOS

DOUGH

300 grams flour
(about 2 ½ cups + 1 tablespoon)

1 teaspoon instant yeast

1 teaspoon sugar

1 tablespoon vegetable oil

140 ml lukewarm water (a little over ½ cup)

nonstick cooking spray

Filling

1 teaspoon ginger

1 teaspoon garlic

½ small onion

2 scallions

½ cup carrot

200 grams (about ½ pound) ground pork
or other ground meat

6½ teaspoons water

1 tablespoon Shaoxing wine
(or dry sherry)

1½ teaspoons soy sauce

3 teaspoons ground bean sauce

1½ teaspoons hoisin sauce

1½ teaspoons oyster sauce

½ teaspoon sugar

¼ teaspoon white pepper

½ teaspoon sesame oil

¾ teaspoon cornstarch

1 tablespoon vegetable oil

MAKE the DOUGH

1. **SECRET #1** Mix together the flour, yeast, sugar, and oil in a large mixing bowl or the bowl of a stand mixer. Gradually add in water while stirring.

2. **SECRET #2** Knead dough very well for about 15 minutes, until it is soft and smooth, like a baby's cheeks. (A mixer with a dough hook works well, but you can also do it by hand if you have the energy.) It should not be sticky or lumpy. When you poke the dough, it should bounce back like a memory foam pillow.

3. Spray a large, clean bowl with nonstick cooking spray, place the dough in it, and turn the dough to coat it in oil.

4. Cover the bowl with a damp, clean towel and set it in a warm place to proof for about an hour. (You can use a slightly preheated oven that's been turned off, or even your dryer after it's run for two minutes and shut off.) The dough should double in size.

MAKE the FILLING

You can make the filling while the dough is rising.

1. **SECRET #3** Mince the ginger, garlic, onion, and scallions and grate the carrot. Put the scallions in a small bowl separate from the other ingredients.

2. Mix the ground meat and 4½ teaspoons of water in a large bowl until smooth. Set aside.

3. Combine the wine, soy sauce, bean sauce, hoisin sauce, oyster sauce, sugar, white pepper, and sesame oil in a small bowl. Set aside.

4. Whisk the cornstarch and remaining 2 teaspoons of water in a small dish until cornstarch is completely dissolved. Set aside.

5. **SECRET #4** Preheat a skillet or wok with 1 tablespoon of vegetable oil, then add the ginger, onion, and carrot. Cook over medium heat until the vegetables soften.

6. Add the ground meat and stir, breaking up lumps. Cook until the meat is no longer pink.

7. Stir in the sauce mixture until well combined, and cook over high heat until most of the liquid has evaporated.

8. Stir the cornstarch and water mixture again and then add to the pan. Cook for a few more seconds while stirring. Remove from heat and stir in minced scallions.

MAKE the BAOS

1. Dust a clean surface with flour and turn out the proofed dough. Knead for a couple of minutes to remove the air bubbles and return it to its original size.

2. **SECRET #5** Make a hole in the center of the dough to create a large donut shape. Evenly squeeze edges of donut while gently pulling to make a circular ring shape. Cut into ten equal pieces.

3. **SECRET #6** Shape each piece into a ball.

4. Using a rolling pin, flatten one of the dough balls into a disk, moving from the outside edge in, so that the outer edges are much thinner than the center. The disk should be about 5 inches in diameter.

5. **SECRET #7** With the dough disk in one hand, place a scoop of filling in the center. Pleat the edge of the dough with the thumb and index finger of your other hand and rotate the bao as you continue to gather and pleat the edges all the way around the top. When you complete the circle, there should be ten or more folds.

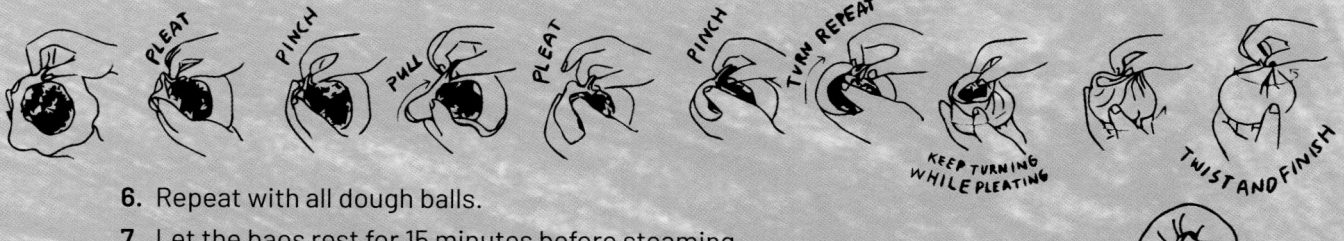

6. Repeat with all dough balls.

7. Let the baos rest for 15 minutes before steaming.

8. **SECRET #8** While they are resting, line a steamer with cabbage leaves or pieces of parchment paper.

9. Place the steamer in a wok or large pot that can hold steamers. Fill the wok or pot with cold water up to the bottom of the steamer placed in the center, but low enough that the water does not reach the steamer slats.

10. Place baos in the steamer on top of the cabbage leaves, leaving about an inch of space from sides and between each bao bun.

11. Turn heat to medium and steam baos for 15 minutes, then turn off heat and wait for a few minutes before uncovering.

You can freeze leftover cooked baos and then steam for 15 minutes from frozen state.

FOR JAMIE AND DENIS, MY FAVORITE BAO EATERS

AND FOR SIMON, WHO FIRST INSPIRED ME
TO WRITE ABOUT LILI'S DUMPLING ADVENTURE

Copyright © 2021 by Melissa Iwai

Printed in China
First Edition

For information about permission to reproduce selections from this book, write to
Permissions, W. W. Norton & Company, Inc., 500 Fifth Avenue, New York, NY 10110

For information about special discounts for bulk purchases, please contact W. W. Norton
Special Sales at specialsales@wwnorton.com or 800-233-4830

Manufacturing by RR Donnelley Asia Printing Solutions Limited
Book design by Kristine Brogno
Production manager: Anna Oler

Library of Congress Cataloging-in-Publication Data

Names: Iwai, Melissa, author, illustrator.
Title: Dumplings for Lili / Melissa Iwai.
Description: First edition. | New York, NY : Norton Young Readers, [2021] | Audience: Ages 4–8. |
Summary: Lili loves to cook little dumplings called baos with her grandmother, but when cabbage is
needed, Lili races up and down the stairs of her grandmother's apartment building to find the ingredient
and help the other grandmothers borrow ingredients for different dumplings, from Jamaican meat patties
and Italian ravioli to Lebanese fatayer and more.
Identifiers: LCCN 2020028265 | ISBN 9781324003427 (hardcover) | ISBN 9781324003434 (epub)
Subjects: CYAC: Grandmothers—Fiction. | Dumplings—Fiction. | Cooking—Fiction. | Chinese Americans—Fiction.
Classification: LCC PZ7.I9528 Du 2021 | DDC [E]—dc23
LC record available at https://lccn.loc.gov/2020028265

W. W. Norton & Company, Inc., 500 Fifth Avenue, New York, N.Y. 10110
www.wwnorton.com
W. W. Norton & Company Ltd., 15 Carlisle Street, London W1D 3BS

2 4 6 8 0 9 7 5 3 1